The God of Elimination

Peter J. Michael

The God of Elimination

This is a Spiritual Fiction Book.

ISBN-13: 978-0-6459234-6-9

Published by Peter J. Michael

ALL BOOKS BY THIS AUTHOR ARE:

THE GREAT WAR AGAINST
TERRORISM

KILLING THE BOGEYMAN I & II

RUTHLESS

RELIGIOUS DEATH TRAP

THE GOD OF ELIMINATION

"And they shall go forth, and look upon the carcases of the men that have transgressed against me: for their worm shall not die, neither shall their fire be quenched; and they shall be an abhorring unto all flesh."
-Isaiah 66:24 KJV
Old Testament

Contents

The God of
Elimination

THE GOD OF ELIMINATION

<u>GOD'S JUDGEMENT</u>

Cursed are all the wicked men.
Cursed are all the wicked women.
Cursed are all your wicked children.

Cursed are all those who say, 'Praise the Lord'
with their tongues, but with their hearts they do
everything that is contrary to my ways.

You think that I created the world for the
wicked to prosper at the expense of the
righteous?

If there is not one righteous person that
remains on earth, you think I will keep the
world going?

I will not keep the world going.
I will destroy the world and everyone who
resides in it.

I look at all the evil abominations of races of people – and I say to myself: This is what horrible wickedness they do to others – so I think what I will do unto you evildoers a thousandfold.

Thus, the creation of Hell.

The bottomless pit which is your ends.

The place of darkness and torture, where I will reign hellfire and damnation - all manner of evil down on you.

You commit evil, so I will bring the most deserving evil upon all your heads!

I will punish you all in the worst ways imaginable!

Those who use their tongues falsely to praise me, will then curse me once they experience their fates inside the bottomless pit.

You will all hate me as I hate you and all you do falsely and hypocritically!

I created hell to punish you unrighteous races of men, women and children.

I created the serpents to bite your flesh.

I created the beasts and demons to tear your bodies apart with swords as your eternal punishment for all your wicked ways!

You killed my righteous followers.

In return, I will destroy you evil sinners.

I created the darkness and the fire which will burn your flesh, but you will never die.

You will live eternally in extreme punishment for your evil wickedness.

You evil races of people killed the last-remaining righteous follower of my laws on earth.

You plotted his death inside a sanctuary you falsely claimed belonged to me.
The Church.

You killed yourselves, but only trapping the final righteous man (that lived) inside your place of ambush, claiming his life with your own.

You think that pleases me?
You think I am happy that this happened?

I am not happy!
I am not pleased!

I am deeply distressed by such a death!

I am deeply angry by such events which
transpired on this evil world called EARTH,
where you all live!

I cannot bear the wicked to prosper on earth at
the expense of the righteous any longer!
I do not tolerate it!
The world cannot continue as this any longer.

I will create powerful winds of change.
Buildings will collapse on your heads, you evil
race of people!

With a strong blast from my nostrils, I will
cause this world and everything in it to topple
over and crush all you evildoers for the crimes
of murder, deceit and falsehood!

You are hypocrites!
You all practise false teachings!

The priests call themselves, Men of God.
You are not, Men of God.
True Men of God do NOT say to the
unrepentant evildoers on earth, 'The Lord
forgives you for murder, for rape, for stealing,

for bearing false witness against others, for all forms of deception and hypocrisies!'

The Lord does not forgive wickedness!

Did I tell you priests that I forgive the unrighteous?
No.
I did not tell you I forgive them.
Nor would I 'ever' say such things.
Yet, you priests are constantly saying the word 'forgive' to those who are not forgiven.
You claim my words falsely.
You use my name blasphemously!

Do you think the Lord is pleased with you evil priests?
No.
I am not pleased.
You evil priests will start dropping dead.
You unrighteous priests will be consumed on earth to enter hell because of your false teachings and false prophecies.

You wicked priests are all damned – both you and your unrighteous followers who enter that place you call Church, to listen and obey your evil words of destructive falsehood and false doctrine!

I will punish you all who use the Lord's name
in vain.

I will punish you all who say the words: 'The
Lord forgives!' when I do NOT forgive.

You put false words in people's minds and lead
all your congregation astray.
You lead them to the path of destruction,
where all you evil priests are headed.

The Lord condemns the wicked priests and all
your immoral followers.

You detestable people pervert everything on
earth.

You call Light-Darkness.
You call Darkness-Light.
You call Evil-Good.
And Good-Evil.

You kill those who do not deserve to die.
And you let live those who do not deserve to
live.
Will I not punish you for such things?
Will I not seek retribution for your dishonest
gains through the perversion of my words?

I cannot bear to see your wickedness any
longer.
I cannot bear to listen to your lies any further.
The strong winds of change thus coming!

****

Robert Stewart was given a choice: to live or to die.
Meaning – to remain dead to a temporary life on a temporary earth.
For the sake of his grieving family, he chose to live.
To return to earth and continue his life of fighting crime as before.

Based on his choice, the powerful-strong winds of change which distressed all corners of the earth had rapidly slowed in intensity, then ceased completely.
Buildings were spared.
The world would continue in existence - for the time being.

Robert Stewart could see his family.
But they could not see him.
Robert Stewart could feel his family mourning for him.
And thus, he made them feel him.

Robert Stewart knew there was still much work in the world that needed to be done.

Thus, his choice of Life ahead of Death!

So, naturally, Robert Stewart maintained his status quo of policing the streets and ridding his city of crime.

****

Upon his return to his house in Brooklyn, he received the most stunned welcome from a very surprised group of family members.
Everyone was shocked to see him alive.
He first revealed himself to his family.
He hugged and kissed them all.
They all hugged and kissed him.
But they were shocked beyond words.
They were weeping until there were no more tears which remained.
They couldn't believe their eyes at the sight of him.
They couldn't believe their ears at the sound of his voice.
Is it you, my son?
Is it you, bro?
Is it really you, Robert?
These were the words of his entire family to him.

Robert was a tough sort of bloke.
He uttered not one complaint of his recent ordeal.
He only smiled to his family in utterance to their question.
He reassured them of the truth with that simple gesture.
That was all they needed to be satisfied concerning the answer to their question.

He certainly was not a ghost.
He was flesh and blood.
He was real.
He stood before them.
And they smiled at the other.
They talked to the other for hours.
And they ate a hearty home-cooked meal for
dinner of Baked Chicken with Spinach Stuffing.
But his family were still shocked.
Imagine what the police precinct and the entire
world would think when they uncovered the
truth? – They all thought amongst themselves.

But Robert revealed himself first and foremost
to his beloved family.
The rest of the world would be told at a later
time!

****

When Robert revealed himself to his fellow police comrades thirty-six hours later, after the initial shock wore off, and the extremely cheerful celebrations to the fact were concluded, it became business as usual.

Robert busied himself in his work – and looked to solve all the new police cases that flooded the police precinct walls.

Robert, for a brief period, was preoccupied by his recent experience.
His recent tragic life's events.
It was sort of nerve-racking.
It really did not take much for a human's life to end.
No matter how well-trained, well-prepared and well-armed a person was, their life could be snatched from them at the most inopportune time!
It was sort of scary.
It almost shook him in a state of panic for a brief period of time.
But he quickly recovered himself and began reading through the many files of new criminal cases that poured into his police office, plunged in a lengthy pile onto his desk.

His 'office', he thought to himself.

His desk.

His name and title: 'ROBERT STEWART - POLICE COMMANDER' were still engraved onto the outside door of his police domain.

It had not been removed during his absence.

Robert could not help but smile briefly to this.

His distraction of thought however would not last long.

It was only brief.

He was sure glad to be back at the station house again.

Seeing all the new police cases waiting to be solved did not bother him.

He was just glad to still be around to solve another police case.

Think of the alternative – he smiled briefly to himself in thought.

And the thought was really humorous.

Who the hell would not find humour in it, even just by the sheer craziness of his recent bizarre Spiritual experience;

For a man, Robert considered himself to be, as not the prayer type of person – and certainly not very religious, even though he was raised by a Catholic family.

Robert considered his recent experience as certainly too indescribable to explain.

And to those who never experienced such a thing, it could be called, 'CRAZY!'
But to Robert, it was a part of the Universe which not many people had seen or experienced with their own eyes and ears before.
It was a reality of truthfulness however.
But to many of those who had not bore witness to this mysterious other foreign world or place or Celestial City – could never really comprehend that such a thing had even existed!!!

Robert Stewart believed a good teacher never teaches anything.
A good teacher only reveals the truth of what already exists!
And the wisdom to know the difference between what is 'manufactured' and what is 'real!'

GOD'S RETRIBUTION

I will avenge myself against all my foes who
arrogantly afflict my people and then use my
name in vain in thus doing so.
The wicked hard-heartedly call themselves
mighty when they kill my people.
They even call themselves God.
They act as if they are the Creator of all things.
They say they are I-the God of the entire
universe.

Do such people have any knowledge?
Do they possess any understanding?
Do they not realise that they are mortal beings?
Do they not know that when I destroy them,
they will blush in shame for ever pretending
and believing that they were God?

When I send them to the pit of hell will these
wicked people still say that they are God?
Will these despicable evildoers yet pretend that
they are doing my work when I bring upon
them all the torments and tortures of the
damned in the universe, for ever tricking the
world with their deceitful vain words and
incorrect beliefs and assertions?

The evildoers are a burden to everything and everyone – and even more so – they kill, steal, rape and destroy the righteous by saying that they are doing God's work.
They falsely claim that I revealed myself to them either in a dream or in person and told them to perform those evil deeds upon my people.
Will I not attack, kill and destroy such evil offenders in all manner of brutal tortures using my deadly weapons of war!

You evil corrupt people put my chosen races in bitter bondage.
But you fail to understand that I will free my people and replace their imprisonment with your own.

My people who are sick will be healed – and the wicked will instead become gravely ill.
My people who are hungry will be filled with the best food and the wicked who are now possessing bulging fattened stomachs will succumb instead to hunger.
The wicked will also learn the unquenchable torments of thirst.

The righteous who grieve for justice will get their wish granted.
And the evil who are laughing at escaping justice for their wickedness, will be eternally punished.
Their diabolical laughter will turn to excruciating sorrow.

Who created the deaf, the blind, the mute and all fatal diseases which afflict the mind and the body – is it not I, the Lord God?
Of course, it was I, the Lord God!

Who created the cures for such diseases?
It was I, the Creator of all things: it was I, the God of the entire universe!
The cures for all brain and body afflictions are right under your very noses.
But you all fail to see.
You all fail to understand the truth.
No one follows the laws of the universe, so the universe is cast against you, hiding the cures from you.

Your evil actions and heinous deeds blind the entire people of the world from knowing the truth.
You cannot see the truth of the one true connection that causes all diseases, including

baldness on your heads, greying of your hair
and old age...
You cannot see because you are all evil.
Your evilness has caused a great barrier which
prevents you from uncovering the truth.
Because the evil is cursed.
I have cursed them.
So, the obvious solutions for all problems
becomes unseen – and your very evil-consumed
and clogged brains fails to see and uncover the
simple truth to all problems.
So, what is simple becomes difficult.
And what remains difficult becomes fatal.

I created the tools to cure all sicknesses, the
same as I have created the means to afflict the
races with such grievous diseases.

But the doctors practise deception.
They do everything within their devious powers
to make money at the expense of their patients'
lives.
They make money by keeping their patients
sick.
They don't want to cure the sick.

The doctors have no real knowledge.
The doctors have no understanding.

They fail to realise that they cannot escape my wrath.
They might escape justice on earth.
But I am The Eternal Justice to all those who have in fact either been robbed by courts of law – or those whom have escaped retribution by the earth's judges.

Judges can be bribed.
Judges can fail to see the truth.
And henceforth, judges who are blind and cannot see the truth clearly, ruling acquittal after acquittal to the unrighteous, is really only just a temporary appeasement to the guilty.

Because I do not acquit the guilty.
I, the God of the entire universe do not pardon the sinful.
I do not grant amnesty to the filthy breakers of my laws.
I do not cast favours unto the evil.
But I will punish the wicked and the evil in all manner of tortures-matching, even far exceeding the manner in which each evil person of the world has sinned.

For instance, when one sins, I will punish that person seven times worse than their sin – and

their punishment will be for eternity, with no
rest, day or night!

You evil sinful people of the world are hard-
headed rebels to what is true and right.
You are all corrupters not only to yourselves –
your bodies and souls – but to the entire planet
earth which surrounds you.
You wicked corrupters of moral laws not only
bring yourselves backwards in calamity, but you
also destroy all those around you, who lack any
sound knowledge to close their eyes and ears to
your destructive actions and words;
But instead choose to follow you as an example
into the gates of hell.

Do you evil people not realise that your houses
and cities and countries are growing isolated.
When I attack you with the sword of
destruction, your lands are truly made desolate
when I reach my hand toward you all, pick you
up and throw you down to the bottomless pit
to be subjected to the worms, the demons, the
fire, the brimstone, the heavy suffocating
toxicity replacing the oxygen on earth, the
darkness, the thirst, the hunger – where the
screams of destruction become the only thing
which occupies you, both of yourselves and the
eternal sorrows of all those damned souls

around you, locked up inside there, all trapped
with you!

Do not commit murder, mass murder, robbery,
theft, rape, extortion and all manner of your
evil abominations, and then have the audacity
to say that you are committing all these evil
actions in my name.

You have also committed a remarkable sin of
blasphemy when you use my name in vain on
top of all your other detestable sins of murder,
mass murder, rape, robbery, theft, extortion,
stealing your neighbour's wife after first killing
your neighbour;
Making lies against your friends because of
jealousy, trying to sabotage your client's success
in his or her work, because you yourselves are
unsuccessful and thus pitifully prone to
destructive acts of jealousy.

NOW, you evildoers who practise all these
manners of wickedness and many more
despicable atrocities upon the righteous, do not
bring forth your hands before yourselves in
prayer.
Because I do not see, hear or listen to the
prayers of the wicked.

But I will only punish the wicked in every brutal fashion necessary in order to satisfy my unquenching wrath against you all for all your evil abominations.

The leaders of countries are all corrupters.
They promise lies to their people.
They sabotage the countries they are reportedly leading through their deceitful ways.
They impose high taxes, which turns its nations of people into lower classes of robbers.
They deceive their countries' people, which makes everyone they lead become liars just like them.
The countries' leaders do not promote harmony by giving its people fair wages for their work, and proper healthcare by insisting that doctors do the right thing by its people, or punishing effectively business people who steal from the work of its talented clients, which only creates a world of talentless idles.

No.

The countries' leaders only help promote disharmony, disunity, rebellion, anger, fury, grievous acts of sin by the people they govern because they – the countries' leaders themselves - are rebellious and evil and wicked and detestably unconscionable in the way they govern their lands - and the selfish, destructive, divisive, even murderous ways in which they govern all those who occupy their cities, states, territories and countries as a whole!

The countries' leaders just serve themselves and not the people, which results in only one ruinous outcome: the destruction of both the leaders of all these countries with all the people they supposedly lead;
Whom will all fall together into the gates of hell where I will send them **'all'** for transgressing against My just laws - and instead of doing what is right, choosing the paths of evil abominations above all else for their own selfish gains.

Where is the justice given by all these leaders to its people?
There is none!

The judges also give erroneous rulings.
They rule in court falsely.
They plot and plan with conspirators behind the backs of everyone.
They accept bribes in order to pervert justice against the righteous by acquitting the guilty.
Will I not punish you for these things, judges?

Will I not distress you all in all manner of evil I shall throw unto your entire beings, far exceeding and outmatching your evil acts and hypocrisies you bestow inside your courts of law you preside inside.

Ah, I will avenge the righteous with my wrathful indignations against the wickedness of all evildoers!

The destruction and death of all evil sinners and unrighteous transgressors of my laws will come to pass in a mighty heap, one by one and together at the same time, when I come after them in my fury and anger, wrath and vengeance in order to consume them all!

And after I have executed all havoc upon them and crippled them from ever committing evil again, will they still say that they are doing God's work?
Will they still say that they are blessed by God Almighty?
Or will they finally realise that they are cursed by Almighty God in an everlasting eternal curse, which will never end in punishing them for their lives of horrible abominations they have subjected not only themselves to, but also all those around them!

The evil are proud and arrogant and they feel mentally and physically strong to conduct their evil deeds day in and day out.

But the proud and the arrogant will become transformed to shame and misery - and the strong predators will become converted to the helpless prey.
From strong and mighty, they will become weak and defenceless, when I come after them and punish the world of evildoers for their wicked abominations!

And they will all be consumed together in an all-consuming fire, that will burn them alive forever and ever and never be quenched!

I will judge these nations of evildoers for all their wicked sins, and I will thrive on punishing them in all manner of mental and physical torments day and night, for eternity!

The evil hide in planes, they discuss their evil conspiracies in submarines or isolated faraway caves.
Do not I, the God who created the entire universe occupy all places, secret or otherwise?
Do I not fill the entire world?

Is there any place on earth that is a secret from Me?
Do the evil and the wicked know that I hear and see everything that everyone says and does at all times of the day and everywhere.
Nothing is a secret from Me!
No evil words or conspiracies to commit murder and mass murder escapes me.
I see everything that you do in all your private planes, underwater submarines and faraway secret caves you enter inside, to discuss your plans of evil in the darkness!

I see and hear everything that everyone says and does at all times.
And I will judge each and every one of you for all your evil conspiracies and actions and punish you all accordingly.

The arrogant and the proud will be brought down.

I will throw the wicked and the mighty down from their mountains, and everyone will look at them in shock and sneer, boo, smirk and whisper at how wrong they were, to ever believe the deceitful words from such people who portrayed themselves as something they were not: a god!

I will crush the mighty wicked ones with my
strong hands.
I will completely destroy and totally abolish the
evildoers from the face of the earth.
I will first spill their blood and expose their
shameful ways to the entire world of passers-
by, who will be shocked at the sight of their
bitter and painful ends I will bring about
suddenly, with my very powerful weapons of
war I will use to attack and kill them all with!

I will cause calamities upon calamities on all
their businesses, homes and residences.
I will shake the entire foundations of the earth
they occupy under their feet - and I will send all
their properties and buildings to fall and crash
down on their heads.

I will punish and destroy the entire world for its
wickedness.
From the countries' leaders, to the judges;
From the privileged of all classes who practise
selfishness, wickedness and hypocrisies.
I will punish the evil priests, pastors and
preachers!
I will punish the young and the old.
I will punish both man and woman for all their
evil sins and detestable abominations!

The wicked will never have a moment's peace and rest from my anger, fury and wrath I will punish them with eternally!

I will oppress all of you evildoers who claim to be honourable when you are not!

The wicked have ruined all four corners of the earth!
And the wicked shall also fall to ruin, because you have all provoked me to anger and fury and vengeance against you all!

Woe, woe, woe unto you evil people.
For the reward of your actions will I repay you all in equal **RETRIBUTION!**

You people practise evil.
And your leaders encourage your evil actions through the evil of their own doings.
Your leaders, as well as the church priests cause you to error in your ways through their own wrongdoings and false teachings!

I will stand before you all and judge each and every one of you outcasts – and I will punish you all according to your ways!

The evil has prospered by stealing, robbing, raping and killing the righteous.
Will I not judge you all for these things?

Will I not attack you all with the blade of a very sharp sword from the crown of your head to the sole of your feet for your wicked ways?

I will avenge the righteous by spilling the blood and killing and destroying the wicked!

The wicked who fill their bellies from the money of the poor will experience tremendous hunger.

The wicked who accumulate their wealth and possessions by all manner of deceit, theft and evil, will have all their belongings stripped from them, and they will lose everything - and finish the course of their lives with nothing but feelings of isolation, misery and despair.

All the evildoers will fall by the sword in the all-consuming outpouring of blood I will unleash upon them, when I exact my vengeance against them all for their wicked ways.

I will declare war against all evil sinners across all corners of the earth!

I will drown you all in a ferocious storm and heavy rain, in order to wipe the earth, clean from the stench of your contaminating existences, which have surely contaminated the world and all the people who surrounded you.

The wicked will be utterly abolished from complete existence.

Not one of you will remain unpunished!

The mean and bad man will be brought down by the sword and the arrogant and the proud will be humbled in the time when I destroy him.

Woe unto the wicked that say his evil is good and the goodness of the righteous is evil!

Woe unto the wicked who bribe the courts to escape justice and pay judges to find guilty the innocent!

I will attack you all unrighteous transgressors in ferocious ways until I remove your existences completely from the face of the earth.
I will force the ground where you stand upon to shake and tremble – and I will open up the

earth and force the vacuum below to swallow you up into the torturous abyss below.

Ah, ye sinners, you shall be broken in pieces in the outpouring of blood I will spill from all parts of your bodies.
I will tear your bodies apart.
I will break your bones.
I will rip and destroy all your flesh.

Cursed are man who put their trust in their fellow man and believe the lies and follies that comes forth from his tongue.
For the deception of man, woman and child will become the dread to all nations of people which occupies all corners of the world!
The wicked are your stumbling block!
The evil are your ruin and complete destruction!
You cannot profit from wickedness forever.
But the punishment for your abominations is eternal.
The evil will be broken.
They will stumble and fall.
All their belongings will be destroyed.
And their followers will become nought.
That is the trap for all the wicked and for all those who follow the evil paths of the heinous sinners.

The words of the wicked have no light in them.
There is no guidance in what they say.
Only death and destruction to those who speak
wickedness and for all those who hear, listen
and follow such evil words into the four walls
of darkness.

The evil are not warriors as they blind the
world to believe.
The evil are sorrowful dead men, dead women
and dead children who meanwhile walk wearing
a mask of demonic righteousness, who will
bring the world who follows them down to
destruction into the ground with them.
All evildoers will succumb to drowning in their
own blood from the open wounds and torn
flesh I will cause them, when I attack them all
with my weapons of war!

The leaders of these people, mixed with the
priests and teachers all speak lies and practise
wrongdoing.
The leaders, priests and teachers have led
masses of people to erroneous paths which
ultimately leads to the complete destruction of
both flesh and spirit!

Therefore, I will have no mercy and no compassion against these people in the day I will punish them with my fury and anger.
Because they have wearied the people with their lies, deceit and false teachings and they have enraged me also by their evil actions and falseness by saying that I, The Living God, blesses them and their evil!
They are all hypocrites and everything their leaders, teachers and priests speak and prophesies from their mouths is all lies.

Feel the wrath of the Lord your God.
For hell enlarges itself daily.
And all the wicked will be consumed in the suffocating dark smoke within its very unescapable secure grim walls.

Slaughter!
Slaughter!
Slaughter!

That will be my very severe actions against you all!
And it shall soon come to pass for all the wicked.
And in your passing, you will become a burden to me no longer!

Because your destruction is necessary!

I will humble you arrogant and proud evildoers
in the day I charge at you with the edge of a
sword!

You mighty ones will all fall.
The predator on earth will become the prey in
the land of your punishment which I will send
you to!

And the arrogant, the ignorant and those with
no righteous understanding in their beings, will
be thoroughly cleansed from all parts of the
earth.
And the world will remain men, women and
children with proper knowledge, wisdom and
understanding.

The wicked will cease to exist!

I, the GOD ALMIGHTY, the LORD
JEHOVAH will completely destroy the tongues
of all wicked liars and false teachers.
And with my strong weapons of righteous
indignation, I will attack, kill, destroy and
utterly consume all manner of evil from the
face of the earth!

I will send the wicked and all their belongings
to a complete and utter destruction.
To absolute ruin!

The hands of the strong shall shake at my
coming!
The black hearts of the evil will tremble at my
approach!
And their spirits will be afraid at the eternal
punishment I have waiting for them, to trap
them inside with chains and shackles on their
wrists and ankles.

All their faces shall be burnt by melting flames
when the LORD cometh after them, to punish
the world for its evil.
Behold, evildoers: the fierce anger of the Lord
cometh forth to attack you all with brutal and
cruel indignation.
I will attack and destroy all evil sinners.
I will make all your evil lands desolate.
I will spill the blood of your wicked seeds and
cleanse the entire world from your dire
carcasses which bears witness to your
existences.

**I, the God and Creator of all things will
punish the entire world for its terrible
iniquities!**

I will kill you all with the sword.
I will cut to pieces your evil children!
I will completely harm and send to death your
wicked wives and husbands!
Not one evil man, woman or child will escape
the fierce retribution of the LORD, your GOD!

So, beware!
Behold…
The LORD is angry at your wicked sins.
The LORD cometh forth to seek retribution
against the evil, for the lives of the righteous
you claimed by your wicked hands!

The wicked will have no rest from thy sorrow I
will inflict upon them for their evildoings!
You will all cease to exist!
Your belongings will become destroyed and
worthless.

The oppressors will become continually
oppressed!

I will execute you all in my wrath!
And all your leaders who ruled your countries
with evil intent and hateful hearts, which
persecuted the innocent, will find themselves
persecuted!

Behold: hell beneath your feet is howling to meet you treacherous evildoers – and all the manner of evil inside that dark place of torture is awaiting your arrivals, to give to you all manner of evil you have inflicted upon others! – for both you and your wicked leaders and sinful teachers.

You will all be cut down and weakened! I will send you to hell the same way you entered this world: completely naked and helpless!

I will purge the earth from the filthy pestilence of you evildoers of iniquity! I will tread you under my foot and squash you down into a dark eternity! I will break the roots of your trees so you can consume no fruit! You will fall by famine! I will dry up the rivers in your lands and cause a tremendous drought to make you die from thirst. I will send wild beasts to attack you and your families and tear your flesh apart with their sharp teeth. I will bring all manner of deadly plagues upon your crops to destroy them. I will make your cattle drop dead at your feet!

I will punish you and your families by bringing upon you all the most painful and deadly pestilence and sicknesses and diseases which you will never be able to cure before it suffocates and kills you!

I will make you stagger when you walk like a drunken man from fright at the sight of all the evil I will cast before your eyes!

And those of you who still remain, will eat the flesh of your children from starvation, and your children will eat the flesh of their fathers and mothers in hunger from the distress and anxiety, lack and suffering I will inflict upon you all, for your evil deeds!

And I will send the rest of you to fall dead into the ground by the sword I will unleash upon you, in the cruelty of my wrath which you have provoked via your wickedness, and then using my name to justify your evil actions against my righteous people!

Your lands shall become a carnage of death, destruction, blood and weeping!

I will execute my ferocious judgements against you, far exceeding your evil oppressive deeds upon my people!

First, I will punish you with all manner of evil torments of the senses and then all the oppressors will be consumed out of this world!

I will destroy your houses with heavy rainfall, powerful storms, strong winds and destructive earthquakes and your occupied lands will become a ruinous heap!

Nothing but desolation will succumb your livelihoods!

Your neighbourhoods will no longer be looked upon as thriving entities.
But you shall call your territories, The Lands of Destruction!

I will remove the burdens of your existences from before my eyes, you evil offenders to the just and the righteous!

I will punish you evildoers in all manner of cruelty and fierceness!
That is MY WILL!

Then I will send you to a terrible place of grievous visions called HELL barefoot and naked, with your buttocks and front parts exposed and uncovered to further increase your humiliation and shame, before all the creatures down below, who will thrive on tormenting and bullying you, you earthly bullies!

It will be like for like!
Evil for evil!
Suffering for suffering!
Death for death!

No mercy for the unmerciful.
No compassion for the uncompassionate.
No reasoning for the unreasonable!

Your former days of laughter on earth will turn to sorrow.
Your health will be turned to weakness.
Your plentiful amounts of food and drink will become hunger and thirst.
Your former earthly pleasures will be replaced by eternal pains.

You will be trodden down violently by a rampage of tormentors in the land of trouble in which I send you!

No more will you call the dishonourable-
honourable and the honourable-dishonourable.
No more will you replace good for bad and bad
for worse.
And you will never again say that the righteous
are evil and that the evil are righteous!

I will bring shame to your pride!
I will lower your arrogance.
I will bring death to your mortal beings.

You tormentors will be tormented!
You oppressors will surely be forever
oppressed!
You evil killers will all perish from this world!
Your earthly homes will become wastelands.
Your lands will become completely empty and
uninhabited.
Your immortal souls will become food for the
worms and for the demons inside the land of
confusion which will become your new home.

Then will you call yourselves, God?
Then will you say that your evil deeds in your
former life were blessed by God?

All manner of evil shall come upon you!

Be ashamed you workers of iniquity!

Be horribly afraid.
You vain of mind and heart are cursed with a
mighty curse of destruction.
I will destroy you!
The unrighteous will yell and scream when I
send my weapons of war against you, breaking
your bones and piercing your flesh.
Your wickedness has polluted the lands.
All your possessions will be burned to ashes.
The fire will consume your bodies.

So don't listen to priests who preach smooth
things to their congregations filled with evil
sinners: murderers, robbers, extortionists,
rapists, thieves, jealousies, wife and husband
stealers, liars, hypocrites, scammers – and all
manner of evildoers who occupy the churches
with false hope and delusions taught by priests,
offering false hope and words of delusion.

Because priests teaching comfortable things
with smooth words to the wicked are deceiving
themselves as well as the wicked.

The LORD GOD does not bestow mercy unto
the unmerciful wicked.
The LORD GOD does not offer forgiveness to
the evil acts of iniquity.

When the priest preaches easy passages and
verses from the New Testament of forgiveness
and mercy to sinners, close both eyes and shut
both ears.
The priest is preaching the delusions of his own
mind to his congregation.
And his congregation are listening with equal
amounts of delusions, in false hope and
complete blindness to the truth.

The priest should not deceive his congregation
filled with sinful men, women and children
saying that the LORD is merciful, forgiving and
understanding to the ways of evil.

The LORD GOD does not forgive evil
practises by the unmerciful.
The LORD GOD does not condone evil
actions by the unconscionable.

Instead, you priests, open your eyes and your
ears and hear the truth of my words written in
the book you preach from.
Stop preaching smooth things from the New
Testament, which hides the truth and conceals
the real motivation behind my actions against
evildoers and their wickedness.

The priests should stop the delusions of fantasy which consumes their minds - and open their hearts to the real truth of reality.

Start preaching my words of truth from the Old Testament.
You tell the evil murderers, the rapists, the robbers, the thieves, the extortionists, the jealous hateful and hated people who try to block the success of the great and talented artists – and all the workers of iniquity - that the LORD GOD will kill and destroy the unrighteous sinner for their evil actions.

You tell the rebellious of heart and the hard-headed arrogant workers of evil, that the LORD GOD will punish the unrighteous at least sevenfold for their evil sins.

The priests should tell their congregations of foolish workers of iniquity that God will surely kill them for their evil sins.
God will punish them in all manner of evil matching and far exceeding the manner in which each individual worker of iniquity has sinned.

So, when the priests preach to their congregations filled with many evil unrepentant

men, women and children – the priests should
say that the Lord God will punish all of you
evildoers for your evil actions.
Speak to them those words, you delusional
priests.
Stop preaching lies and words of fantasy which
perverts not only my words, but my intentions.

If a man, woman or child commits evil intent,
the priests should say, that the LORD your
GOD will surely punish, destroy and kill that
evil person and persons for their evil.
The LORD GOD will surely send all manner
of wicked punishments against the wicked.
The wicked will surely die for his and her
iniquity.

Do not listen to any priest who preaches
forgiveness and mercy to the
UNRIGHTEOUS.
Did I speak to the priest?
Did I tell the priest that I forgive the villainy of
the wicked?
Of course, I did not.
I never told the priest in any vision or dream to
say those things - and yet the priest preaches
false words in my name which I never said nor
would I ever speak such words in relation to
the wicked.

So why is the priest speaking words in my name which I never told him to speak?
Nor would I ever speak the words forgiveness or mercy in regards to the unmerciful evildoer.

The priest must guard his own words and motivations carefully.
The priest must serve as a teacher of truths to his congregation, not a preacher of deceit, lies, falsehood and delusions, in order to make money, by promising empty promises of forgiveness and mercy to his congregation filled with many evil sinners.

Only listen to my words of The Living God which speaks the truth and they are: The wicked will be punished severely and will be completely destroyed for his and her evildoings!
I do not pardon the iniquities of the unrighteous sinners.

There will be no peace for the evil!

And once the wicked are all consumed, I will restore the earth with judgement and justice once again!

GOD'S BLOODLETTING

I kill and I make alive.
But for the wicked, there will only be despair,
sorrow, destruction and unending torments,
forever and ever.
I will attack the unrighteous with my sword of
fury.
The wicked will have his flesh and bones
slashed and crushed on all sides.
The wicked will feel the blade of the sword
cutting off his thumbs and his toes.
The unrighteous will have severed his arms and
his legs.
The spear will cut out his eyes and his nose.
And I will smash the teeth of all evildoers.
The land will be filled with the red-coloured
blood of every practitioner of evil.

Will the evil still laugh with his evil laughter
saying: We have gotten away with what we did.
We have destroyed the LORD's followers –
and the LORD did nothing about it.
We have raped the wives of the righteous.
We have also gang-raped their wives on all
sides by entering all their holes at the same
time.

No one heard us when we gagged her screams.
We have defeated the righteous do-gooder in all
our perverse ways.
We have robbed all his belongings.
We killed his children with the axe.
We stole all his family's money.
We burnt his house to the ground.
We stole his artwork creations and we stole his
ideas and then we sold his artwork as our own;
By replacing his name on his creations with our
names.
We lied.
We stole.
We killed.

We became rich by our unrighteous deeds
against the LORD's followers.
We defeated the righteous in all our wicked
ways.
We executed their wives.
We killed their children.
We took all their possessions.
We committed all manner of evil against the
despised righteous.
We did all that because we were allowed to do
it.
And where was God?
Where was he?

He was obviously asleep and not paying attention when we committed all acts of evil against his people.

We killed them with the knife.
We killed them with the sword.
We killed them with an axe.
We killed them with our guns and with our bullets.
We put them in the grave with our fists of wickedness.
And God who saw **not** what we did, will not do anything about it.
He will forgive us our evil sins and he will forget what we did, when he sends us to PARADISE, upon our deaths, when we finally leave this very evil world of ours.

****

Is that not what you will say, evildoers!
But I, the LORD, will see everything and has
seen everything that you have done.
I have surely witnessed 'all' your wicked
abominations.
And I will not pardon your evil iniquities.
I will not let the unrighteous be acquitted from
his evil deeds.

But instead, I, the LORD GOD, will turn the
lands where your feet tread, into the blood of
your corpses, when I kill you with all my
powerful weapons of war, I will attack you
with.

Your foolish evil laughter will turn to tears of
blood and grievous sorrow.
Your joy will be transformed to unending
misery.
What you have stolen will never benefit you.
Because I will set on fire all your possessions -
and you will lose everything you have possessed
from robbery and evil.
I will slay your wives.
I will slay your children.
I will slaughter your animals.
I will cut the flesh of your arms and your legs
with my sword, with my axe and with my
strong hands.

I will shed your blood as you have shed the blood of my people.
I will make your foolish senses dead from all feeling.
I will cut out your eyes.
I will cut off your ears.
I will remove your nose and your hair and your clothing before your enemies.
And you will want to run away in shame, but you will not be able to.
Because you will have no legs to run away with. You will have no arms to claw yourself into a place in the dirt to hide from ME and your enemies I will encircle you with, until they destroy you.
I will bring fire on all the lands around you to burn your possessions.
Your wives and children will be burnt alive at the stake.
I will fill the land with the blood of all my enemies when I slaughter you wicked sinners for the bloody slaughter and butchery you have committed against my people.

Then will you say that the LORD does not see your sins?
Then will you say that the LORD does not hear your evil words?

Will you also say that the LORD will forgive and forget your sins when I bring grief and misery, death and destruction unto you all for eternity inside the gates of hell where I will send you?

When you are screaming every moment of every day and every night for eternity from the horrible torments I will subject you with, what will you say then?
You cannot say that the LORD is merciful to the wicked, any longer.
You cannot say that GOD forgives your evil sins, can you?

But what you will realise when it is too late for you evil sinners, is that the LORD takes much pleasure and satisfaction at the wrathful vengeance I hence seek and exact against you unrighteous foolish followers of the devil.
You horrible devil worshippers will surely suffer a horrible end, with the devil as your companion, in the land of death and destruction I have condemned you to, forever and ever and ever and ever!

I will attack and destroy the wicked in many unbearable ways, far outmatching and greatly exceeding your evil deeds.

I will utterly slay to death the guilty and the
wicked.
I will bear witness to the lands you possess,
which I will turn red with your blood, when I
destroy you limb by limb with my weapons of
war, in the day of the brutal unleashing of your
brutal punishments and painful deaths!

I will kill you with fire.
I will kill you with the sword.
I will kill you with the flood.
I will execute you with drought.
You will die from starvation.
I will shatter and smash your heads and bodies
with my hammers.
I will smash your teeth so you cannot utter
another guilty word.
I will sever your bodies limb by limb, so you
will never be able to sin another guilty deed
again.
Then I will slaughter you!
You will never reign over the righteous again.
But the righteous will bring grief, and more
grief will they subject unto you, than those you
inflicted upon the righteous.
The righteous will slay you in my presence.
And I will be satisfied.
They will destroy the flesh of your bodies.

And then, I will seek eternal retribution and vengeance against your souls in the place of misery, darkness, fire, despair, torture, weeping and gnashing of teeth, in which I send you to!

The evil men of bloodshed will experience all the evil and bloodshed you will all succumb to by my hands.
With my breaths of fire, I will slay the wicked to death…to death…to death!!!

I will make you all die painfully for your careless conducts, you horrible evil sinners.
I will throw dung on your faces.
You will eat the flesh of your own families in hunger.
I will force you to eat the excrement of your enemies, you wicked evildoers!
I will set your homes and possessions on fire.
I will force you evildoers to die by the sword, the axe, drought, famine, disease, horribly painful pestilence and mass-destroying plagues.

Your names will become a curse to all those lives who remain among the living on earth.
Everyone who lives, will curse you before and after ME and my servants slay you to death.
Your names will be forever cursed in shame.

The wicked are not only evil, but they are
foolish.
Their ways often resemble rebellious children.
They do not see the light.
They are only blinded by darkness all around
them.
They do not know me, God.
Yet, do they say, the LORD forgives and
forgets their wickedness.
Do you not hear my words?
Do you not understand what I am saying?
The Lord loves righteousness – I hate the evil.

I will never forgive your sins.
But I will triumph gloriously when I obtain
honour against the unrighteous in the day, I will
make you fall dead onto the ground in
destruction, as punishment for your wicked
ways!

I am the strength and you workers of iniquity
are the weakness.

I am the Almighty God of war.
LIGHT is my name.
And DARKNESS is the punishment I will
subject all the wicked to, in the day I will inflict
misery and death unto you all!

I will bring heavy rains and destroying thunders
to cover you until you drown.
I will attack you with hail and lightning.
I will cause the mountains and the hills to
collapse onto your heads.
I will bring all the wild beasts of the earth and
deadly creatures of the sea to attack you with
their sharp teeth, until your evil carcases are
forcibly removed from the world!

**With my axe and with my sword, I will dash
you in pieces.**

And with the greatness of my sanctity, I will
make sure the evildoer never rises again, when I
consume every wicked man, every wicked
woman and every wicked child from the face of
the earth, to cause you vile people intentional
horror, terror, anxiety, dread, fright, panic,
alarm and hate, when I come after you – and
attack you with my vengeance and indignation,
in my ever-consuming wrath!

**I will reduce you to ash and bones into the
ground, you wicked ones.**

And finally, the blood I spill from your flesh,
covering all the lands for all your enemies to see
and bear witness, will finally be cleansed from

the earth by the rain I will force to wipe away
all the pestilence of your existences, finally!
Yes, finally!

I will divide your lands and possessions, to be
taken over by your enemies, evildoers!
My hand will strike you.
My sword will cut you in pieces.
And I will finally destroy you all!
I will destroy your planes.
I will sink your ships.
I will collapse your houses with mighty
thunders and powerful rains.

The wicked will be utterly consumed when I
force the world to swallow them up!

In the day of your slaughter, the unrighteous
will succumb to becoming very afraid and
sorrowful, struck with unending grief and
misery, when I punish them with no mercy and
no compassion – but, with eternal fury and
anger for provoking me with your evil ways.

The evil will be forced to tremble when I attack
them with my deadly weapons.
And finally, I will bring a fire unto them, which
will melt them away into the earth, forever and
ever!

Behold, evildoer: fear, dread, despair, misery, death and destruction cometh forth to consume you.

I will destroy you in the day I inflict punishment upon punishment against you unrighteous souls, with the greatness of my powers.

For the wicked are like wood and I am the fire that will burn the wood to ash.

There will be no safe haven for the wicked. There will be no sanctuary for the unrighteous. There will be no peace, but only torments for the evildoer, forever and ever and ever and ever!

I will reign upon the righteous as I will punish the wicked, for eternity!

The evil thinks he will prosper.
But the ungodly has no knowledge or understanding of the truth.

Only I, The LORD GOD, will triumph in my glory and excellency against the wicked, when I slay them with the sword and cut their flesh and bones in pieces in the day, I subject the unrighteous to a complete death and destruction.

The priests speak follies and lies.
The prophets are all false, saying the Lord has spoken to them in dreams and visions, telling them to commit evil against the righteous.
The preachers preach blasphemy.
The world's leaders teach its people wrongdoing, and they commit acts of evil when they say that what is good is bad and what is bad is good.
All men, women and children are prone to erroneous ways.
Is there no end to man's evil deeds?
Will I not visit the world for their evil in the day of their destruction?
Of course, I will surely visit man, woman and child in the day of their bitter punishments I will bestow upon them for enraging me to acts of anger, fury and vengeance because of their wickedness!

The evil has compounded sin upon sin in my name.
You are all blasphemers!

The wicked kill, rape, steal, rob, commit
extortion, extend loans with high interest – and
then they strengthen their evil hearts by asking
solace and forgiveness from evil priests who tell
them lies, saying: The Lord God forgives you!
So, the unrighteous feels compelled to walk out
of the church confessional to keep sinning!

Will I the LORD not bring an end to an evil
world as this?

The evildoer has no shame!

The wicked priest has no understanding of
what he preaches when he says to the evildoer:
The Lord forgives your continual sins of
murder, mass murder, rape, robbery, extortion,
loans with high interest rates, killing your best
friend in order to steal his desirable wife, and
committing blasphemy in my name.

So therefore, the evildoer will not only die in
his sins, but he will also lose his soul on
account of the wicked priest who speaks
blasphemy in my name.
And because the priest is compelled to commit
acts of blasphemy for reason of evil gains
through money and sinful gifts by the wicked,
the priest will also be condemned to death and

his soul will burn for eternity in hellfire and
brimstone;
The place of despair and destruction I have
created as my gift of punishment to the wicked
and the ungodly evil man, woman and child
horrible sinner!

From the tallest to the shortest will be punished
for his and her sins.
From the lowest to the highest will be
consumed by his and her iniquities!
From the lowest-ranked worker of the land to
the highest-ranked leader of countries will
suffer the punishment, in the day I will seek
revenge against all evildoers for his and her acts
of wickedness in my name!

So do not listen to the priests' lying tongues or
the false prophets' false dreams and false words
in my name.
And do not listen to false preachers and
deceitful teachers whose lying words will not
only bring the wicked to a greater fall, but the
lying priests, false prophets and false teachers
and lying preachers will also succumb
themselves to a bitter calamity of death and
destruction as well!

The strength thy wicked seeks from thy priests will become thy shame.
The lies spoken by the tongues of priests, preachers and false prophets will bring no profit to one's soul.
Only misery, despair and death!
ETERNALLY!

False words and a lying tongue will become the shame to those who speak such follies and deceitful words.

The liars and the hypocrites will be subjected to the burdens of the beasts, who will bring you destruction, trouble, sorrow and despair, when they attack you with their sharp claws and piercing teeth to tear your bodies to pieces.

The wicked will be tormented by the vain words he and she speaks - and/or he and she listens to - and follows, through the follies of others and their false directions.

The mighty man will be brought into the ground in the day of my visitation, when I visit the earth to punish all the unrighteous and the ungodly for their evil actions and wicked words which speak destruction against my people!

You evil people of the world put your trust in words of a perverse nature by perverse people. You believe in oppression spoken by oppressors!

You have no understanding between the good and the evil.

You do not see the difference between the light and the darkness!

No!

You only listen to evil words spoken by practitioners of evil, because all the people are lovers of evil themselves!

The mighty evildoer will be brought low and henceforth will no longer be able to fool those around him by saying he is mighty in the day of his reckoning at my will!

No!

But the mighty and the strong will flee from fright when I chase him with my weapons of war, to rebuke and punish him as he has rebuked and punished my people.

The wicked will run and hide.
But because I fill all of the earth, the evildoer cannot escape the punishment I have ready for him.

Because I will raise the low, as I will throw down and crush and destroy those who sit on high, committing acts of destruction and speaking words of deceit to the world!

And when the wicked leader is brought onto the ground in the day of his fall, when calamity and destruction strikes him, it will become a sign to all other evildoers, whose confused minds will be forced to concede that their mightiness is only a figment of their delusional thoughts, but the truth is, all evildoers are the fallen ones.

All the unrighteous will never have a moment's peace, only they shall succumb to eternal suffering!

Behold, ye unrighteous ones: The Lord cometh down from very high above to punish the world of evildoers with my burning fury and unquenching anger, my breath of fire and bringing forth the powerful weapons of my arsenal against you.

The Lord God Jehovah is my name, coming to attack you all with what is called: **GOD's BLOODLETTING,** vexation, hatred, displeasure, resentment, violence, rage, animosity, scorn and destruction drawn against you evildoers, filled with my eternal indignation and unending wrath!

The day of my vengeance is near.
I will breathe a fire of death unto you.
I will draw the sword from its sheath and spill your blood from your head to your foot.
I will break your necks.
I will break your bones.
I will tear your flesh apart.
The mighty arrogant ones will be utterly consumed.
The proud and the laughing evildoer will become ashamed and sorrowful in the day I punish him, when he falls!

And the righteous who witness the death and destruction of the wicked, will experience a gladness of heart, to smoke their tobacco and drink their wine in comfort and solemnity.
The righteous will sing a song of justice in the day of the evildoers' calamity, death and destruction awaiting him and her!

The day of the wicked one's fall will show the LORD's hand of indignation, anger and fury brought against the evil.

There will be thunders, hailstorms, earthquakes, fire and all manner of natural calamities which shakes the world beneath the feet of all evildoers, making their hearts tremble in fright, as I force them to drop dead onto the ground in punishment for their evil sins that has been a burden unto the world from its conception! And they have been a burden unto me!

I will smite the wicked with a rod and I shall devour the evildoer with the sword, in the bloody fight and deadly battle I will wage against all the unrighteous who are polluting the world with their pestilence and deceit! I will cause the earth under their feet to shake, then will the earth mysteriously open up to swallow like a vacuum all unrighteous souls into the abyss below, which awaits their eternal punishments!

Yes.

In the day of your punishment, the vile person will no longer be called righteous, nor will the righteous be called vile.

The earth's lands will no longer be filled with evil leaders, false teachers, false prophets, wicked priests and corrupt judges who rule rulings of villainy unto the righteous, acquitting the wicked with rulings of perversions of justice.

The lands filled with no judgement and no justice against the wicked, will be replaced by true judgement and true justice against all evildoers and their evildoings!

The evil will no longer prosper in his and her evil ways!

The evil will no longer remain guiltless for his and her guilt!

But the evil will be mocked, condemned and have the blood spilled from all the veins of his and her bodies, for their misdeeds.
And the truth that the evil is evil will be cast forward before all man, woman and child to bear witness to the truth.

And the evil will no longer call himself mighty.
And the righteous will no longer be persecuted by the wicked!

But the wicked will be made lower than the
dust!
And the righteous will be brought up higher
than the mountains.
And justice will be served.

**There will be Death to the wicked who will
weep bitterly and Life for the righteous who
will laugh gladly!**

GOD'S BUTCHERY

I have witnessed all the evil abominations of the people of the world, and the people have also seen the evil punishments I have repaid both the wicked sons and the wicked fathers and the wicked fathers of fathers and many ancestor forefathers, going back 3-4-5-6-7-8-9-10 generations before you.

The fathers and the sons have done evil before my eyes as have the mothers and the daughters. And I have and will continue to repay your evil actions with extremely evil punishments I will manifest against you all, as I have manifested my anger and wrath against your very wicked ancestor fathers and ancestor mothers before you – and forefathers and foremothers before them!

You rebellious, evil sinful transgressors have continuously provoked me to anger and wrath against you.
And the punishments have always been forthcoming against you loathsome men, women and children!

As I have done unto your detestable fathers and mothers, I will do fervently unto the villainous sons and the daughters of this generation.
I will crush and destroy the minds, bodies and spirits of all who provoke me to my actions of anger, wrath and vengeance against you all.
The punishment will be unleashed against you filthy evildoers thick and fast!

For all you murderers, assassins and homicidal maniacs, I will attack you all with a painfully mortal, fatal, lethal and death-dealing punishment.
I will slay you with the sword.
I will execute, strike and massacre you evil men, women and children with a powerful axe.
I will destroy, slaughter and wipe out the many nations of wickedness by butchering you all to pieces, cutting your flesh and making you all drown in the outpouring of blood from your torn flesh and veins.
You evil assassins will be massacred by my powerful blows to be delivered against you.

I will unleash a horrendous killing-spree against you vile people.
I will slaughter you all in a very gruesomely painful fashion.

Those inclined to committing homicide will be struck by a deadly homicide!

I will unleash my destructive weapons of war against you, which will result in a non-stop massacre and bloodbath carnage, which will attack and destroy your flesh and bones.
I will incorporate the bloody killings and slaughterhouse annihilations of every evil repugnant being across all nations.

No one will escape my fierce and gruesome punishments against them!

I will create a carnage filled with your dead bodies onto the streets outside your living quarters, for all passers-by to witness and hiss, boo and laugh at your butchered massacred corpses.
I will force the world of survivors to mock you. You evil butchers will become a laughingstock when I slaughter you all in a very gruesome fashion for all your victims to witness.

I will incorporate the savage killing of a very large number of evil rebellious people across all nations.

That day will become the day of your humiliating massacres and vengeful butchery to deaths and justifiable defeats!

A very cruel killing-spree awaits you evil wicked men, women and children of the world.
I will prepare a bloody slaughter against you all. I will unleash a catastrophic massacre of your lives for all your victims and enemies to bear witness to my vengeance against you all!

I will cut you up and hang your dead body parts from a tall tree to be eaten by the wild birds until your dirty carcasses rot away.

I will slaughter you evildoers and leave your dead bodies onto the ground for the dogs to eat.

And I will sink your ships and force you to be thrown into the ocean, where the sea creatures will attack you with their sharp teeth and eat you alive!

You abhorrent, repugnant, repulsive, detestable men, women and children will become targets for my vengeful wrath against you!

You hateful and repulsive people will be killed
by a mighty slaughter at my hands.

You abhorrent, revolting, disgusting two-faced
hypocrites will be identified and revealed to the
world.
Your devious back-stabbing actions will be
known by all and sundry.
You vile, obnoxious, horrible, loathsome
people will be humiliated on the day I destroy
you in the time of your bloody slaughter.

You are appalling, dreadful, awful, evil workers
of cowardice.
I will repay your evil actions with painfully evil
punishments for all time.

Your actions of evil are vile and offensive and
my punishments against you will be greater in
ferocity and magnitude.

I will crush your skulls and break the bones of
your bodies.

I will turn the lands of your heritage red with
your spilled blood!

I will execute you inside your homes!

I will send the wild beasts of the world to attack you with their razor-sharp claws and tear your flesh off your bodies with their sharp teeth.
I will send giant animals to trample you with their feet and crush your bones.
Then I will be completely satisfied at the sight of your mortal crushed corpses being mixed with your spilled blood.
And after your gruesome deaths, I will bear witness to the destruction and punishments of your immortal souls in the special place of torture I have prepared for you all: every evil man, woman and child to endure forever and ever!

Your evil sins and wicked abominations will be repaid in full.

I will send the bees in swarms after you to attack your skin and sting you.
I will send the wild birds to attack your head and body with their beaks.
The wild animals of the earth will satisfy their hunger by eating your flesh and bones.

Your enemies will attack you with deadly weapons.
I will send your enemies to rob your houses.

I will cause a heavy wind and storm to destroy your mansions.
I will attack your cattle and crops with a deadly plague.
I will send your wives, your husbands, your children and your evil friends to the slaughter.
I will burn all your buildings and possessions into the ground.
I will attack you evil offensive people with a gruesomely painful pestilence.
You will experience a severe itch of the skin.
I will cause you to have an unbearable fever!
You will get blotches of the skin.
You will experience painful blood and pus-filled massive boils.

I will attack your throat and stomach with very deadly sicknesses.
You will lose your appetite.
I will cause you to die from extreme hunger and thirst.
You will drop dead in despair, misery and torment also by the afflictions caused to your husbands, your wives and your children, as well as your partners in crime.

My punishment against you will be bestowed unto your mortal beings on earth, and once you are removed from the earth by death, I, the

LORD GOD, will attack your souls down below for all eternity!
Punishments upon punishments awaits you loathsome workers of iniquity.
It will result in a double destruction to you all, on all fronts!
So be prepared and get ready.
Because death and destruction cometh forth, you filthy detestable enemies of mine!

My weapons of war are dripping with your blood.

My weapons of war are stained with your torn flesh.

My axe and my sword are smiling with gladness at your deaths and destructions, O wicked fiends of the world!

Your deaths are imminent.
Your destructions are certain.
Your punishments are inevitable!
Your torments are justifiable.
Your sufferings are retribution.
And your screams are for me a very much personal revenge!
As the wicked thrive on committing evil abominations, I, the LORD GOD, thrives on

killing, destroying and savagely punishing you offenders to me and my followers.

As you evil cowards commit sin and laugh at your victims, in the day I punish you all, those victims will become witnesses to your butchery and executions, and you will be a laughingstock amongst all men, women and children, your former victims and targets!

And I will be completely satisfied at the sight of your butchered corpses on earth, those mortal beings – and I will also be completely gladdened by the sounds of your eternal screams of brutal torments and tortures of your spirit flesh, those immortal souls, FOREVER!

Because I am a God of war!
I enjoy punishing the wicked!
I enjoy their sufferings and torments!
After all, I am the creator of all that is good and all that is evil!

As I have created the good things, I have also indulged in the practises of evil things, prepared for all the evils of the world and going back toward generations of evil, from the beginning of man's creation!

I bear witness to the punishment, suffering, misery, torture and torments of the evil damned souls at all times.
I witness their stunned eyes.
I listen to their groans of pain and torture.
I read the thoughts of their excruciating anxiety-fuelled minds.

I have employed many hero prophets throughout the generations to destroy such wicked men, women and children on earth.
But I take pride in my own handiwork and heroic deeds in punishing the wicked.
Because my creative ingenuity is unmatched.
No one can entertain the superior methods of torture, death and destruction against the wicked better than I, the LORD GOD of the entire universe!

My prophets have always been guided by my invisible unmatched powers of force and brutality against the wicked, in finalising their deserved slaughters.
But my beloved prophets as my dreaded evil enemies all combined since man's evil creation, could never equal and compare or outmatch and surpass my methods of brutal torture, death and destruction against my enemies.

My ingenuity and uniqueness cannot and will
not ever be outperformed.
I can never be eclipsed.
Because I am the God of the universe.
Is there any other God but me?
Of course, there is no other God but me.
No one is my equal.
Which means, my goodness is eternally
unmatched as is my evil actions against the
wicked will also be forever unrivalled!
My tortures and punishments against the
loathsome offenders of my will, can never be
imitated!

My evil punishments far exceed and far
outweigh even the rottenest villain's and most
fiendish villains' actions all combined in the
history of man's repugnant life on earth!

I am God who created all and sundry!
Which means no one can compare to my
unique goodness as no one can compare to my
justifiable evilness!

As a lion is made to roar and attack against his
prey, I am forced to acts of vengeance against
this world filled with iniquitous, crooked,
rotten, evil-minded, vile people.

The priests and pastors are all prone to blasphemous lies in my name.
The deceitful preachers and false prophets are all guilty of damning masses of souls into the fire and brimstone below.

The teachers and country leaders are sinful and immoral.

Those who call themselves experts are all frauds.

Those who claim to be healers of the sick are only harming their patients in order to line their pockets with great sums of money.

Is this a world that I should take pride in its people and their actions?

No.

This is not a world that I should feel any pride or pleasure or satisfaction in man, woman or child's vile accomplishments.

Because the people have only accomplished one thing: they have mostly provoked me to actions of extreme vengeance, retribution and punishments against them by fuelling my anger, fury and rage towards them because of their very disgusting sick actions against me and my followers!

So, my evilness is ignited against a world contaminated by dirty rotten wickedness and filthy repulsive evildoers.

I will attack the mind, the body and the spirit. I will give those evildoers very grievous and painful afflictions all over their entire beings.

I will attack their minds.
I will poison their bodies.
I will torture their spirits.

I will kill their wives, husbands and children.
I will slaughter their evil friends.
I will cause an earthquake and a flood to destroy their belongings and kill their cattle at the same time destroying their crops.

I will cause them madness diseases of the brain. They will succumb to a deep depression and anxiety of thought.

I will give them blindness of the eyes.
I will cause them deafness in the ears.

I will smash their teeth and force them to cut
out their tongues so they will remain forever
mute.
I will cause inflammatory diseases of the brain
and the body.
They will succumb to blood circulation diseases
causing their hearts to stop beating.

I will give them tumours and spreading deadly
cancers that no human will have the ability to
heal.

I will cause the wicked, diseases of the skin.
They will develop blotches, blemishes,
abnormal growths filled with blood and pus
and excruciating pains.
I will force them to have no peace even when
they relieve themselves.
I will cause diseases of the male and female
genitalia, so when they urinate, they will
experience severe discomfort and bleeding.

They will be struck by very painful
haemorrhoids.

Their stomachs will become afflicted with
constant feelings of fullness so they cannot eat,
causing wasting diseases.

I will cause unexplained afflictions of the nervous system that will paralyse the muscles of the entire body so they cannot walk or move any part of their arms and legs.
Diseases which are mostly obtained at old age will be given to young-and-old alike!
Instead of a full head of hair, you will have baldness.
Instead of perfume, you will stink!
Instead of clear skin, you will be covered with visible large blemishes from head to foot.
Your wagging tongues will be smitten, so you cannot speak.
You will die mute.

You evildoers who are of shifty arrogant eyes, deceitful lying tongues, minds and hearts that mischievously concoct wild and deviously evil schemes, hands and feet that are prone to attack the innocent, committing crimes such as killing, rape, murder, extortion and all other heinously selfish acts - and those hypocrites and two-faced scoundrels who tell lies and spread false rumours about people as false witnesses, in order to cause conflict and chaos against others and stir up strife and division in the cities, states, countries and your neighbourhood communities at large – you evil hypocrites will face my bitterest judgments and you will be forced to suffer extreme destruction of the mind, flesh and spirit forever and ever, with no rest, day or night!

And I want the world never to forget my incomparable goodness for the righteous and my unequalled evilness against the wicked!

GOD'S WARFARE

I will roar in a mighty rage against the immoral,
the bad and the wicked people of the earth.
My slaughter of multitudes of evil wrongdoers
will be provoked because of the vile,
unpleasant, malicious, destructive and hateful
actions of a great number of evildoers.
I will strike my deadly weapons of disdainful
enmity and scornful conflict in all four corners
of the world.
My powerful massacres will slaughter every
malicious and nefarious man, woman, child and
beast that lives on this earth.
Not one wicked person will escape my bitterly-
fuelled vengeful wrath and hostile rebukes
against them.

The disgusting, the dreadful, the diabolical
wickedness of man will be repaid in full when I
spill his blood before his evil family and friends.

The sinister, the foul, the loathsome devil-
worshippers who have provoked me to extreme
anger will be crushed, destroyed and forced to
finally perish from off the face of the earth.

I hate your evildoings.
I rebuke your vile thoughts.
I despise your villainous words.
I dread your cowardly behind-people's-back
conspiracies.
And I detest utterly the blasphemous ways in
which you satanic-worshippers' sin, by using
my name as a reason to sin.
You have dishonoured and disrespected my
glory.
And I will repay your blasphemous ways with a
great slaughter I have prepared against you
iniquitous, vicious and destructive vile people.

By your evil hands and actions, you have
provoked me also to acts of destructive, cruel,
brutal and barbaric retaliations against you all.
I will smash your heads and bodies onto the
concrete ground you stand upon.
I will crush your bones and tear your flesh
apart.
I will damage, defy and destroy your shameful
and offensive evil, by bringing a great and
painful slaughter against you and your wives
and husbands and children and friends who are
co-conspirators in your heinous crimes against
my people and against me, the LORD GOD of
the entire earth!

You foul, distasteful and appalling people will
succumb to a bloody end;
A very gruesome slaughter.
A vengeful massacre will strike you all…HARD
and SWIFT!
A sickening death awaits you repugnant and
vicious people.
A torturous demise will be thrown down on
you.
Every imaginable painful slaughter and
vengeful agonising means of death will be
prescribed against the wicked.

You loathsomely corrupt and viciously
malevolent people will be killed with a very evil
slaughter by my hands.
I hold you all in a perfect contempt and eternal
hatred for your vile wrongdoings you have
performed against me and my people.

Your villainy is contemptible and your
blasphemy is an abhorrence.
I abhor and despise you blasphemers who
commit all acts of detestable atrocities and in
doing so, you attempt to purify your guilty
consciences by saying that your evil acts are
'what God wants,' and, 'what God intends.'

And worst of all, you claim that your detestable loathsome abominations were, in your own words: 'Ordained by God!'
You claim that I have told you to commit such evil and foul actions and mischievous rancorous deeds.
You claim that I bless your wicked malevolence.
And the priests also claim this as well every time they forgive your acts of wicked sins inside the church confessionals, by granting you dirty foul evil people absolution for your reprehensible sins, borne by a lack of conscience and remorse.
I will punish, destroy and absolutely kill you all for such evil abominations against me and my people.
By teaching such heinous lies, the evil villains of the world have caused many of their weak followers to believe these absolute slanderous falsehoods in my name – and as a result, not only will the foul-mouthed teller of these lies be destroyed, but all those followers of you detestable people will also be cast forth into the fiery pit below – and all and sundry will be consumed into eternal damnation.
And the priests who have taught the world such blasphemous lies will also lose their horrible miserable contemptible souls as well!

I will punish the world for their abominations.
No one will be spared!
Murder, death, slaughter, destruction and
misery awaits you vile offenders of my just
laws!

You will die in a river of blood;
The blood flowing onto the earth will be your
blood.
The blood of every deserving contemptible
person will be spilled onto all corners of the
earth, you detestable wicked men, women and
children, who will die a terrible death with the
beasts of the universe.

Mothers and fathers: - curse your evil children.
And children: - curse your evil mothers and evil
fathers.
Everyone: - curse your evil friends.
And for all and sundry: - curse and condemn
the wicked priests who taught you to
blaspheme and sin in my name, offering
absolution for your evil sins, where I would
never absolve the guilty.

Curse and destroy one another.
Treat your friends and families with hateful
contempt.

Because it is your families and your friends who are your greatest enemies, who lead you entirely to erroneous ways and false beliefs.
And the priests who prophesy lies and falsehoods in my name will be totally consumed.

Destruction upon destruction upon destruction will strike the heads of all the wicked on all corners of the world!
Misery upon misery upon misery awaits you all!
Suffering upon suffering upon suffering will strike everyone who has provoked my vengeful anger and wrath against them!
Death upon death upon death awaits you malicious and horrible blasphemers of the world!

The heinous transgressors will weep and mourn when I strike them with instruments of steel and iron across their heads and bodies as punishment for their loathsome actions!

With heavy rain, great hailstorms, strong winds and all-consuming fire will I destroy and burn down your homes.
I will devour all your possessions.

Your residences will become places of desolation with no one to be found anywhere in such territories.

I will break the heads of all evildoers and cut off the wicked inhabitants of the world and cast them into eternity below.
A place of great sorrow and torture awaits you workers of iniquity!

For all your sins in my name, the punishments will be forthcoming!
I will deliver you all to captivity, depravity, fire, deadly weapons pointed at you striking you hard in lethal blows and into the grave below!

I will be fully satisfied at the bloodshed being spilled from your bodies, you wicked men, women and children, with beasts!

I will bring my hand against you, striking your heads and bodies – then you will perish.

I shall pursue the abominable unrighteous wicked ones with the axe, with the sword, with fire, with brimstone and I will tear your bodies apart in my anger and wrath forever, with no mercy, no compassion and no withholding the severe punishments against the total sum of the workers of evil covering all four corners of the world!

My wrath will be kept forever!
From the smallest of you to the tallest.
From the lowest-ranked to the highest-ranked members of society will be utterly consumed in my rage against you, because of your evil deeds!

Leaders of countries, the rich, kings and queens, priests and pastors and all your servants and followers who practise evil iniquity, will all be led to the slaughter!

Rich and poor, young and old, will be subjected to destruction because of their evil deeds!

The corrupt doctor and the bribed judge will be utterly consumed by the fire!

Those who gained their riches by unruly dishonest gains will be made to perish and their possessions will be destroyed.
And in hell where I cast you, then you can reflect on what use your stolen possessions had given you into the place where I will send you.

The bullies on earth will be bullied in hell below!

The tormentors on earth will be tormented in the flames below!
The torturers on earth will be tortured in the dark place below in which I send them!

Not only will your lives perish from total existence, but so too will I kill your wives, your husbands, your children, your friends and your animals closest to you!
Double-and-triple destruction awaits you evil sinners!
A gruesome massacre, a bloody slaughter and a terrible death will succumb the loathsome vile despicable evildoers on earth!

First, I will slaughter your mortal bodies, then, I will torment your black souls forever!

Blood, weeping, gnashing of teeth, fire, brimstone, the worms and the demons are the monumental traps I have in store for the evil and the wicked!

No one is exempt from my wrath!
The rich and the poor.
The kings and their servants.
The queens and their staff.

The doctors, the judges, the false prophets, the lying priests, the hypocritical two-faced pastors, the deceitful preachers with the crooked leaders of countries, states and territories who practise covetousness and iniquity, will be totally and fully eradicated, when I subject them to the bloody slaughter for their evil ways!

The evil believe they will escape the punishment.
But what if I reveal to everyone via my prophets, that those evildoers condemned to death make up a very large number of many individuals – and only a few people will be saved who are righteous!

The evil constantly and daily attempt to trap the righteous – but I, the LORD GOD, has an even greater trap in store for the wicked.

As I stated before: human evilness does not compare to the great heights and masterful ferocity of the evilness designed by me: the LORD GOD!

I will punish each person for the evils they have committed in their hometowns and the wicked actions they have performed within the walls of

the territories, cities, states and countries in
which they have sinned.

The oppressors will be forever oppressed!
Violence, robbery and murder will strike against
the violent robbers and murderers!
The strong will be weakened and the fattened
belly will be replaced by skin and bone!

I will visit the evil of the world in the day of
their punishment, death, destruction and
calamity which awaits them very soon!

I will strike their knees with heavy iron bars and
they will fall to the ground, screaming in bitter
agony when I spill their blood and break their
bones!

And I will smite their evil children who smile to
their evil parents saying: 'Thank you mother
and father for teaching us all the evil things we
will inflict on the world around us!'

When I say that those members of one's family
are their greatest enemy, no truer words have
ever been spoken.
The mother and the father are the child's first
tutors.

And whatever the parents teach, the child, in most cases, will usually follow.
So, the mother and father are responsible for the life or the death of the child's soul.
So surely, and most certainly, the evil parents are the worst enemies to their very own children!
Because not only will the evil mother and the evil father be destroyed, but so too will the evil child who listens, follows and obeys the evil thoughts, words and deeds of the evil parents!

It is the same as the wicked priest's teachings to his congregation.
If the wicked priest tells his disgraceful and shameful congregation that rape, murder, acts of robbery, extortion and all manner of double-dealing hypocritical evils, are sins worthy of forgiveness, then not only will those heinous members of the priest's congregation be subjected to the slaughter, but so too will the priest himself be sent to death, because of his careless foolishness and hypocritical deceitful evilness, in casually teaching the masses who enter his church everything that is incorrect - which will ultimately consume the body and the soul in death, of all those who listen and follow such dreadful and deceitful instructions!

So, if you want death to follow you, listen to the words of liars and deceivers - and the slaughter of both the body and the soul will surely transpire!

The wicked practitioners of deception will come to nought.
They will all be crushed and made to perish as dust in the ground!
The riches will be taken away from all evildoers as well as their posterity, their sanity and the mental and physical health of all the wicked!
Ye shall all be cast unto eternal destruction.

I will smash your teeth, remove your tongues, cut out your eyes and your ears and send you completely into a place of utter darkness and despair, where you will succumb to total madness, which will satisfy my desire for vengeance against you as punishment for your evil actions!

As I cause it to rain in one city and place, I will withhold the rain from your properties, so you will be subjected to thirst and famine when your rivers dry up and your crops die from the drought!

I will send all manner of natural disasters
against you and your homes.
First, I will destroy your livelihoods by giving
you drought and famine!
Then I will send your houses crashing to the
ground when I force a heavy rain to pour down
on your residences, with crushing hailstones
and destructive winds, that will destroy you and
your properties with terrible floods and your
houses will fall down!
Everything you own, all your possessions, will
be devoured.
That is the trap which awaits the evildoer!
I will send enemy armies to attack you with
their deadly weapons.
You and your families with your friends and
cattle will be led to the slaughter.
The blood from your torn bodies and the stink
of your dead corpses which will fill the lands of
your-then destroyed homes and properties, will
rise into the nostrils of all passers-by, who will
start hissing at the horrors they begin to
witness.

I will overthrow the proud, the arrogant and
the delusional mighty into shame, horror and
absolute destruction!
The mountains will fall on you, the winds will
blow you onto the ground and the darkness

which will succumb your existences will shatter
your eyes with blindness and force your
collapsed bodies never to rise again!
Your destructive ends cometh forth thick and
fast and no one will help you, O fiendish one.
Because I have destroyed your evil friends and
your evil families as I will destroy you with the
bloody and destructive slaughter!

In the day of your fall wicked ones, you shall
never rise again!
You have profaned what is good with what is
evil!
You have brought to shame what is good
judgement and replaced it with wicked bribes,
unscrupulous dishonesty and grand larceny!

**You criticise what is great by saying that
greatness is bad and bad is greatness!**

Can you hide your manifold evils from me in
your dark places you enter with your cohorts to
discuss your plans of robbery and murder?

NO!

You cannot hide from me.
I fill all the earth, the sky and the seas.
No place is invisible from me.

I bear witness to all your mighty sins against the righteous and I see your secret envelopes given to you filled with dishonest bribes, in exchange for heinous deeds of deception and lies!

Where are the prudent of the world?

Where is the righteous?

I look and find only a few, because the world is filled with workers of iniquity: it is an evil time!

I will force the lands to shake and tremble in the day of my visitation in punishing the wicked of the earth to a ferocious death!

I will force the wicked to face the black day which will be their destructions, when they mourn for their evil deeds only outmatched by my very evil punishments against them!

I will send their enemies to slaughter them inside their own homes – and all the wicked will fall dead onto the ground that day: which will be the day they all drown in the dark sea of their own red blood!

I will send the waves of the sea to crash down on them, when I replace the sun and the moon with bitter black darkness: the sign of a dark day: a black day of doom, death and destruction against the wicked!

I will turn your crops into weeds and your fat bellies will become hungry when I fill your eyes with mourning, distress and lamentation.

Your mouths will open but there will be no food to eat nor water to drink.
I will force you to faint from the lack of all life-giving sustenance.

I will destroy the repugnantly sinful. The wicked will soon die and they will never rise again!

That day will be a day filled with my anger and wrath, vengeance and rage to cause misery, distress, darkness and slaughter against all evil man, woman and child which fills the earth.

I will throw dung on the faces of all the workers of iniquity.

Through their evil thoughts and evil actions, they will be consumed with the very powerful might of my great reprisals and agonising punishments, as I spill their blood from their butchered bodies, and force their intestines to pour out onto their polluted lands.

I will create a hefty riddance of all the evildoers and their riches from existence.

I will bring forth a decree of retribution against all the wicked inhabitants on all four corners of the world, who have provoked me to anger and retaliation!

I will proceed in a terrible attack against all the horrible on earth.

The destructive, hateful, malicious, vile, destructive and awful, loathsomely corrupt villains will experience famish in all its forms.
I will stretch out my hands against the evils of the world and attack them with terrible evils I will throw right back into their faces.
I will send the roofs on their houses collapsing onto their heads until I crush them completely.
All their animals will fall dead onto the ground bitten by a brutally deadly plague.
The pestilence will consume their children as the children's parents will be consumed with a deadly curse, I will strike them with on all parts of their bodies, from their heads to their feet.

And the righteousness of the righteous will rejoice at the deathly end of the wickedness of the wicked.

The villainous people who have polluted the cities and countries with their filthiness will be torn apart.

The snake-infested leaders of countries and arrogant wolves who call themselves judges, with the frauds who say they are healers in medicine and all workers of soul-destroying witchcraft and sorcerers will be consumed in a ferocious death.

The deceitful false prophets, treacherous pastors and lying priests who have brought wrongdoings and pollution to many people's minds with false teachings which provoke violence and blasphemy in man – such despicable fraudulent prophets, pastors and priests will also succumb to bitter ends filled with violence, misery, despair and total death and destruction against them!

The streets of the earth will be filled with the corpses of the wicked who have no shame. I will punish all their corrupt doings with no end to the onslaught against them.

My determination is great, and my indignation is strong just as my punishment against the wicked remains forever unmatched.

My fierce anger directed at the evil of the world will consume all such despicable men, women and children from the face of the earth with all manners of evil and the fire stemming from my rage.

Once the evil is consumed and removed from the earth – there shall be no more lying tongues, deceitful words, obnoxious thoughts and diabolical actions;
Because the reign of the evildoers of the world will cease to exist by my very strong hands in the day, I descend down to strike at them, attack them and kill them totally and completely, sparing no one!

And in the glorious day of the absolute downfall of all evildoers, the righteous who will remain in the world will sing songs of gladness and rejoice merrily at the sights they see: the eternal destruction of the wicked.

All that afflict the righteous will be torn apart in eternal afflictions!

The wicked will have their entire bodies burning as an oven in the flames!

The dreadful will be burnt to dust and ashes and will exist on earth no longer!

The righteous will tread down the wicked with the soles of their feet until the evildoers are dead onto the ground and rise no more!

The unrighteous will be overthrown and will become much like dung onto the side of the streets!

The evil man, woman and child conspire to pursue the righteous in all manner of abominations, but the despicable will surely be overtaken to result in a great slaughter, when I stretch out my hand on earth and destroy them – then the earth below will swallow them up into the pit and the snare underneath the world!

The wicked will succumb to weeping sorrow, fear and dread when the fire below melts them into oblivion!

The great shall become small, the arrogant will become humble and the proud will be ashamed!

Will you commit fiendish acts such as blasphemy, witchcraft by means of cursing and bringing death to the righteous, false prophesy, civil offenses consisting of crimes against man, woman and child, homicide, robbery and larceny, assault and mayhem, sex crimes as rape, malicious prosecution of the innocent and perjury, torts, kidnapping, property damage, abusing one's honourable authority by committing dishonourable acts hypocritically, oppression of the underprivileged without being sent to the slaughter.

NO!

You will not commit fiendish acts such as blasphemy, witchcraft by means of cursing and bringing death to the righteous, false prophesy, civil offenses consisting of crimes against man, woman and child, homicide, robbery and larceny, assault and mayhem, sex crimes as rape, malicious prosecution of the innocent and perjury, torts, kidnapping, property damage, abusing one's honourable authority by committing dishonourable acts hypocritically, oppression of the underprivileged without being sent to the slaughter – by stoning, by the axe, by the sword, by mutilation, by scourging, by burning, by enslavement and eternal imprisonment and by all forms of evil I will bring down upon your heads!

The wicked are not only evil, disgusting and foolish, but also, they are delusional.

When someone asks, why does the good die young?
It is simply for one great purpose: to spare the righteous ones from the evils to come.

When I say that the wicked are not only evil, disgusting and foolish, but also, they are delusional – it is because the wicked are trapped by the ignorance of their own minds.
They commit all manner of evils, unaware that their very acts of evil deeds will be the result of their doom and despair!

I control the true justice systems of the universe.
Trust not in man or woman to deliver true justice!
But the LORD GOD is the ultimate justice: the eternal justice!

I am the salvation of the righteous as well as
the destruction of the wicked!

For all the loathsome, detestable,
abhorrent, malicious, sinister, cruel and vile
wrongdoers prone to evil acts of immoral,
devilish, destructive, heinous, nefarious,
awful and disgusting villainy – I will send
upon you in vengeful retribution a
disastrous treatment consisting of great
suffering - which entails brutal torture,
ruthless torments, terrible misery and
eternal damnation, forever and ever with no
rest, day or night!